THE WRITINGS OF THE
GREAT BEAST

SOME SHORT STORIES

BY ALEISTER
CROWLEY

British Library Cataloguing-in-Publication Data
A catalogue record for this book is available from the
British Library

CONTENTS

INTRODUCTION

TO

THE WRITINGS OF THE GREAT BEAST: SOME SHORT STORIES

by Aleister Crowley

So much has been written about Aleister Crowley, and so much of it born out of sensationalism and speculation, that one hesitates to pen a single more word on the man and his work. Whatever the merits of 'The Great Beast' as a thinker and writer, his voluminous body of writing has been almost totally overshadowed by the even more voluminous body of biographies, anecdotes and parodies which surround him. To confuse matters even further, Crowley's public legend is a highly polarising one: To the British tabloid press, he was "the wickedest man in the world," guilty of an array of horrors ranging from coprophilia to child abuse. At the same time, in a 2002 BBC poll of the '100 Greatest Britons',

Crowley placed 73rd, ahead of Geoffrey Chaucer and Sir Walter Raleigh.

In this light, this collection will concern itself with the biographical details of Crowley's life only as far as is necessary in order to contextualize and illuminate his writings. He was undoubtedly a fascinating man – by turns a rock-climber, chess master, classicist, poet, astrologer, traveller, magician, and even British spy – but proper, extensive treatments of his colourful life are available at great length elsewhere. Instead, *The Writings of the Great Beast* will deal as directly and as objectively as it can with a section of Crowley's oeuvre that has over time been somewhat ignored: his short fiction.

Despite being better-known for his lengthy tomes on the topics of Thelema (his spiritual-religious philosophy) and *magick*, Crowley was writing prose and poetry years before he published any non-fiction. While studying English literature at Trinity College, Cambridge, Crowley was a prolific producer of verse. His earliest notable publication, *White Stains* – a work of poetic erotica which had to be published pseudonymously in Amsterdam in order to avoid the British authorities branding it obscene – appeared in 1898. In November of this same year, at the age of 23, Crowley joined the Hermetic Order of the Golden Dawn. A magical order active in Great Britain during the late 19th and early 20th centuries, the Dawn has been credited with being of the largest single influences on 20th-century Western occultism, and it was Crowley's experiences as a member of the order that provided the inspiration for a number of his future short stories.

In 1907, following a less-than-amiable split with the Hermetic Order of the Golden Dawn, Crowley co-founded the magical order A∴ A∴.. Two years later, he began to publish *The Equinox*, a series of biannual publications in book form that served (and, in fact, continue to serve) as the official organ of the A ∴ A ∴.. Billed as "The Review of Scientific Illuminism", *The Equinox* was the publication in which Crowley published much of his early short fiction. More broadly, it was the springboard for his (somewhat half-hearted) attempt at serious fiction-writing. Indeed, it was between the founding of *The Equinox* in 1909 and the outbreak of World War I in 1914 that Crowley produced virtually all of the short fiction which appeared during his lifetime.

It is fitting, then, that the first story in this collection – 'At The Fork of the Roads' – was first published in Vol. I, #1 of *The Equinox*, in the spring of 1909. In his *Confessions of Aleister Crowley*, the 'Great Beast' called the tale "a true and fascinating story of one of my early magical experiences," and – unsurprisingly – it relates to a personal feud Crowley became involved in while a member of the Golden Dawn.

As biographers of Crowley's such as Richard Kaczynski have uncovered, the central events of 'At The Fork of the Roads' mirror an incident that took place in the summer of 1899, when Crowley was visited by Irish poet and artist Althea Gyles. Gyles was a close friend of the famous Irish poet W. B. Yeats, and had drawn the covers for a number of his early poetry collections. Yeats and Crowley, meanwhile, as fellow members of the Golden Dawn, were bitter enemies. According to Crowley, at the close of Gyles' 1899 visit, after a short discussion of clairvoyance, she scratched him with her brooch as she left his house. The next day, again according to Crowley, she admitted to him that Yeats was attempting to use black magic to destroy him.

Upon knowing these facts, the curiously personal-sounding language used to condemn the absent yet dastardly 'Will Bute' comes into focus: ". . . the long lank melancholy unwashed poet . . . Will Bute was not only a poetaster but a dabbler in magic, and black jealousy of a younger man and a far finer poet gnawed at his petty part." Over the course of Crowley's life, these sorts of carefully crafted criticisms of thinly veiled acquaintances would become an almost constant feature in his fiction.

'The Dream Circean' appeared in Vol. I, #2 of *The Equinox*, during the fall of 1909. The tale is set in Paris – a city Crowley visited frequently, and lived in for at least two extended periods, including during the twenties – and concerns itself in part with painting, another of his part-time pursuits. In his *Confessions of Aleister Crowley*, Crowley declared that the story was written at a times when he "was incurably sad about Rose." Rose Edith Kelly, who Crowley married in 1903, was at this time – Christmas of 1908 – suffering heavily from alcoholism and related dementia, and Crowley had recently fled her company after finding himself unable to cope with her diminished state. The monomania which lies at the heart of the story, and the sad tale of Frédéric (who, like Crowley, finds himself inspired by the French occultist Eliphas Lévi), can therefore be seen to have strong autobiographical overtones.

'His Secret Sin' is the first of the three stories in this anthology which make up the only collection Crowley produced during his life time: *The Stratagem and other Stories* (1929). However, 'The Secret Sin' was actually originally published many years earlier, in Vol.1, '8 of *The Equinox*, during September of 1912. Based on an idea given to Crowley by friend and fellow writer Victor Benjamin Neuburg, it is a darkly amusing tale, concerning, as Crowley put ut, "a prosperous English grocer in Paris . . . who wants desperately to be 'wicked', but is ashamed to inquire how these things are done." Eventually, the grocer plucks up the courage to buy an "indecent photograph," and what follows, with relation to his daughter, is disastrous for him. It is worth relaying, at length, what Crowley himself stated of the story in his *Confessions*, as it gives good insight into both the tale itself and its author's own world-view:

This tale is one of the most bitter truths that I have penned. I am glad to say that it is almost the only evidence of what I felt with regard to the attitude of the English bourgeoisie towards art and sex; and, even so, my picture of the younger generation bears witness to my unshakable faith in the emancipation of my folk. Indeed, I have not wrought in vain. The young men and women of today, generally speaking, are as free from superstitions and sexual shame as I would have them. It is only a further proof of this that the "old guard" are more desperately narrow and fanatical than ever. They are trying to stop drinking, smoking, dancing and reading, by law. Intolerance is evidence of impotence. (*Confessions*, p.667)

'The Testament of Magdalen Blair' was the second, and longest, of the three tales which comprised *The Stratagem and other Stories*. First published in Vol. 1, #9 of the A∴A∴'s official organ, *The Equinox*, it is regarded by many as Crowley's single best short story. He described the genesis and development of the story himself as follows:

The best short story, as some think, that I have ever written belongs to 1912, "The Testament of Magdalen Blair". The idea was based on a suggestion of Allan Bennett's made in 1899, and fallow in my mind ever since. It was this. Since thoughts are the accompaniments of modifications of the cerebrial tissue, what thoughts must be concomitants of its putrefaction? It is certainly as ghastly an idea as any man could wish for on a fine summer morning. It thought I would use it to make people's flesh creep. My difficulty was how to acquaint other people with the thoughts of a dead man. So I made him a man of science and provided him with a wife, a student at Newnham, endowed with extraordinary sensibility which she develops into thought reading. She and her husband make a series of experiments and thus develop her faculty to perfection. He gets Bright's disease and dies, while she records what he thinks during delirium, coma and finally death. I managed to make the story sound fairly plausible and let myself go magnificently in the matter of horror. I read it aloud to a house party on Christmas Eve; in the morning they all looked as if they had not recovered from a long and dangerous illness. I found myself extremely disliked! (*Confessions*, p. 687)

In its delving into the psyche of the dying, decaying psyche, 'The Testament of Magdalen Blair' is highly reminiscent of

Edgar Allen Poe's 'The Facts in the Case of M. Valdemar', in which a mesmerist hypnotises a man at the exact moment of his death. It even echoes it in the fact that Poe's tale was originally thought to be a scientific report, and publicised as such, and Crowley failed to get his story published in the *English Review* because the editor "required proof of its literal truth." The fact that this story – and a number of Crowley's others – are strongly reminiscent of Poe is perhaps little surprise when one considers that Crowley declared that "Poe and Whitman are still in my opinion the only first-rate writers until very recent years."

'The Strategem', the title story of Crowley's only prehumously published collection, first appeared in *The English Review* in June of 1914. The response it received from the publication's editor, Joseph Conrad, saw Crowley come as close as he ever came to turning wholeheartedly to the writing of fiction. Once more, the background to the story is worth reprinting at some length, in Crowley's own words, as laid down in his *Confessions*:

I had a bad attack of influenza, which settled down to very severe bronchitis. I was visited one evening by an old friend of mine and her young man, who very kindly and sensibly suggested that I should find relief if I smoked a few pipes of opium. They accordingly brought the apparatus from their apartment and we began . . . My bronchitis vanished;

I went off to sleep; my guests retiring without waking me. In my sleep I dreamt; and when I woke the dream remained absolutely perfect in my consciousness, down to the minutest details. It was a story, a subtle exposure of English stupidity, set in a frame of the craziest and most fantastically gorgeous workmanship. Ill as I was, I jumped out of bed and wrote down the story offhand. I called it "The Strategem". No doubt it was inspired by Jupiter, for it was the first short story that I had ever written which was accepted at once. More: I was told---nothing in my life ever made me prouder---that Joseph Conrad said it was the best short story he had read in ten years. (*Confessions*, p. 721)

As it was, following the minor buzz caused by the publication of 'The Strategem', Crowley spent fifteen years in the US and Sicily, focussing once more on scholarly approaches to Thelema and *magick*. By 1929, when Mandrake Press published *The Strategem and other Stories*, as well as his novel *Moonchild* and his autohagiography *Confessions*, if Crowley had ever had a window in which to become a fully-fledged fiction writer, it had gone. (Or, perhaps more accurately, Crowley had left it.) The attempt from Mandrake Press to rehabilitate and kick-start his writing career came too late, at a time when in many people's eyes Crowley was already 'the wickedest man in the world', far removed from such measured pursuits as the production of serious literature.

The final two pieces in this collection are short extracts from the aforementioned *Moonchild*. Written in 1917, *Moonchild* – originally titled *The Net* – is Crowley's best-known novel. Its plot involves a magical war between a group of white magicians, led by the protagonist Simon Iff, and a group of black magicians, over an unborn child. Crowley ends the book's Author's Note with the playful "Need I add that, as the book itself demonstrates beyond all doubt, all persons and incidents are purely the figment of a disordered imagination?" However, as he states in his *Confessions* (p.776), "most of the characters are real people whom I have known and many of the incidents taken from experience." (Indeed, such a blatant self-contradiction, aimed largely at entertaining himself, is typical of Crowley's writings on his work and life.) The novel itself is occasionally dense – Crowley, as he put it, "give[s] an elaborate description of modern magical theories and practices" – but if one has patience, it is an engaging and interesting read, its abrupt end notwithstanding.

The first of the two extracts is Chapter XV of *Moonchild*. It carries the expositional and lengthily title "Of Dr. Vesquit And His Companions, How They Fared In Their Work Of Necromancy; And Of A Council Of War Of Cyril Grey And Brother Onofrio; With Certain Opinions Of The Former

Upon The Art Of Magick." Despite being a chapter of a wider work, it works excellently as a standalone piece, and an examination of a practice Crowley presumably had first-hand experience of. As context, it is worth noting that Crowley himself was – despite what many believe, thanks to his over-inflated public legend – a staunch opponent of necromancy (or what he termed 'spiritism'). In Chapter 21 of his *Magick in Theory and Practice*, entitled 'Of Black Magic', he stated the following:

All spiritists . . . feel dirty even across the street; their auras are ragged, muddy and malodorous; they ooze the slime of putrefying corpses.

No spiritist, once he is wholly enmeshed in sentimentality and Freudian fear-phantasms, is capable of concentrated thought, of persistent will, or of moral character. Devoid of every spark of the divine light which was his birthright, a prey before death to the ghastly tenants of the grave, the wretch, like the mesmerized and living corpse of Poe's Monsieur Valdemar, is a 'nearly liquid mass of loathsome, of detestable putrescence.'

The student of this Holy Magick is most earnestly warned against frequenting their séances, or even admitting them to his presence. They are contagious as Syphilis, and more deadly and disgusting.

The second *Moonchild* extract is Chapter XIX, entitled

'The Grand Bewitchment'. (Discerning readers will spot the reappearance of Abdul Bey from Chapter XV.) Important context for this piece – and for the entire novel, in fact – is the concept of the 'black lodge' within occult thinking. Perhaps originating with Russian occultist H. P. Blavatsky, the 'black lodge' is a derogatory term used to refer to competing lodges, orders, or even ideologies. Crowley, meanwhile, tended to use the term 'black lodge' to refer to Christianity as a whole, or even to the more general mental and spiritual obstacles he encountered during his life and development. Additionally, the 'apaches' referenced in the early part of the chapter were a turn of the 20th century Parisian subculture associated with crime and debauchery, and the ancient Greek goddess Hecate was a figure of the underworld adopted in modern times as a goddess of witches.

I had begun, I do not in the least remember how, to try my hand at short stories. Even today having written more than seventy such, I do not quite understand why this form of art should appeal to me. I take fits of it. I go for a month without thinking of the subject at all, and then all of a sudden I find myself with ideas and writing them down. I entirely agree that the short story is one of the most delicate and powerful forms of expression. It forms a link with poetry because one can work up to ecstasy of one kind or another in a more lyric manner than is possible in a novel; the emotion evoked is doubtless more limited, but it can be made for this very reason better defined. (*Confessions*, p. 438)

Short fiction was never Crowley's first love – indeed, even poetry absorbed more of his attention – and yet he undoubtedly appreciated the form, and turned his hand to it seriously on a number of occasions. In the past thirty years, something of a revival of this neglected section of his oeuvre has been taking place, and more of Crowley's short stories have now been anthologised more than was ever the case during his life: *Simon Iff, The Big Game* (1985) and *Scrutinies of Simon Iff* (1987) collected Crowley's attempts to reach a truly mass audience through accessible and witty detective tales he wrote during World War I. *The Scented Garden of Abdullah the Satirist of Shiraz* (1991), originally published as just 200 copies in 1910, features explicit accounts of homosexuality – extremely bold, when one considers that Oscar Wilde had gone to prison barely a decade before its original appearance. Even more recently, *The Drug and Other Stories* (2010) includes nineteen short stories never even published during Crowley's life.

A sporadic, dilettantish fiction writer, then, but not one to be ignored outright. Few would disagree with Crowley when he says that "the short story is one of the most delicate and powerful forms of expression" – whether he succeeded in doing the form justice is up for debate. Just like his public persona, Crowley's writing was a polarising force. In their review of *Moonchild, The Sheffield Independent* cited an "unusual measure of genius" and *The Times Literary Supplement* praised its "literary skill." The *New Statesman*, meanwhile, declared "Possibly the author may know what this nonsense is all about." Readers shall have to make up their own minds.

AN EXPERIMENT IN NECROMANCY

ALEISTER CROWLEY

The Neapolitan winter is one of uncommon clemency at most times, but in the year in which our story occurs even this state of affairs had been surpassed; indeed save for a touch of frost, kindly and wholesome, on a few nights, it had no frown or rigour. Day after day the sun enkindled the still air, and life danced with love upon the hills.

But on the night of her fullness, the moon was suddenly tawny and obscure, with a reddish vapour about her, as if she had wrapped herself in a mantle of anger; and the next dawn broke grey with storm, the wind tearing its way across the mountain spine of Italy, as if some horde of demon bandits were raiding the peasantry of the plains.

On one ridge particularly subjected to the senseless madness of the blast stood the villa of a certain occultist, one Dr Vesquit, who had come especially to this isolated region for the performance of a most terrible and dangerous experiment in necromancy – the operation for making contact with the spirits of the dead.

As the day passed, the violence of the storm increased and the Doctor began to fear somewhat for the safety of his plans. Then, dramatically, about an hour after noon the speed of the hurricane abated and the sky was visible, through the earth-vapours, as a wrack of wrathful clouds.

Though the gale was yet fierce, its heart broke in a torrent of sleet mixed with hail; for two hours more it drove almost horizontally against the hillside, and then, steadying and steepening, fell as a flood, a cataract of icy rain.

The slopes of Posilippo roared with their foaming load; gardens were washed clear of soil; walls broke down before the impetuosity of the waves they strove to dam; and the streets of lower Naples stood in water to the height of a man's thigh.

The hour for the beginning of the work of the Doctor w

as that of sunset; and at that moment, much to his relief, the rain, after a last burst of vehemence, ceased entirely; nightfall, though black and bitter, was silent as the grave.

In a little chapel behind Dr Vesquit's villa where the ritual was to take place a portion of the marble floor had been torn up; for it was desired to touch the naked earth with the bare feet, and draw her powers directly up from their volcanic stratum.

ONE OF ALEISTER CROWLEY'S
NUMEROUS SYMBOLS

This raw earth had been smeared with mire brought from the swamps of the Maremma; and upon this sulphur had been sprinkled until it formed a thick layer. In this sulphur the magic circle had been drawn with a two-pointed stick, and the grooves thus made had been filled with charcoal powder.

It was not a true circle; no figure of sanctity and perfection might enter into that accursed rite; it had been made somewhat in the shape of an old-fashioned keyhole, a combination of circle and triangle.

In the centre of this shape lay the body of a man which had been secured for the rites by trusted and well-paid functionaries, its head towards the north; beside it stood the first of the Doctor's assistants, a tall, thin fellow named Arthwait, who held the mystical *grimoire* in one hand, and a lighted taper of black wax in the other. On the opposite side was a second man, a Turk, Abdul Bey, holding a goat in leash, and bearing the sickle which the Doctor was to use as the principal magical weapon of the ceremony.

Dr Vesquit was himself the last to enter the circle. In a basket he had four black cats; and, when he had lighted the nine small candles about the circle, he pinned the four cats, at the four quarters, with black arrows of iron. He was careful not to kill them; it was important that their agony should frighten away any undesirable spirits.

All being now ready, the necromancers fell upon their knees, for this servile position is pleasing to the enemies of mankind.

The forces which made man, alone of all animals, erect, love to see him thank them for that independence by refusing to surrender it.

The main plan of Dr Vesquit's ceremony was simple; it was to invoke the spirit of a demon into the goat, and slaying the animal at that moment of possession upon the corpse, to endow that corpse with the demoniac power, in a kind of hideous marriage.

The object was then identical with that of spiritism, or 'spiritualism', as it is commonly and illiterately called; but Dr Vesquit was a serious student, determined to obtain results, and not to be duped; his methods were consequently more efficient than those of the common or parlour medium.

The assistant, Arthwait, opened the *grimoire* and began his conjurations. It would be impossible to reproduce the hideous confusion and complexity of the manner, and undesirable to indicate the abomination of the matter. But every name of opposition to light was invoked in its own rite; the fearful deities of man's dawn, when nature was supposed to be a personal power of cruelty, delighting in murder, rape, and pillage, were called by their most secret names, and commemoration made of their deeds of infamy.

Such was the recital of horror that, cloaked even as it was in Arthwait's unintelligible style, the meaning was salient by virtue of the tone of the enchanter, and the gestures with which Vesquit accompanied him, going in dumb show through all the gamut of infernal discord, the music of the pit. He showed how children were cast into the fire, or thrown to bears, or offered up in sacrifice on bloody altars; how peaceful nations were uprooted by savage tribes in the name of their demon, their men slain or mutilated and enslaved, their women butchered, their virgins ravished;

how miracle testified to the power of the evil ones, the earth opening to swallow heretic priests, the sun stopped in the sky that the hours of massacre might be prolonged.

It was in short one interminable recital of treachery and murder and revenge; never a thought of pity or of kindliness, of common decency or common humanity, struck a false note in that record of vileness; and it culminated in the ghastliest atrocity of human history, when the one man in all that cut-throat race who now and then showed gleams of a nobler mind was chosen for torture and death as a final offering to the blood-lust of the fiend.

With a sort of hellish laughter, the second conjuration continued the recital; how the demon had brought the corpse of his victim to life, and mocked and profaned his humanity by concealing himself in that man-shape, thence to continue his reign, and extend his empire, under the cloak of hypocrisy. The crimes that had been done openly in the fiend's name, were now to be carried on with fresh device of shame and horror, by those who called themselves the priests of his victim.

By this commemoration was concluded the first part of the ceremony; the atmosphere of the fiend, so to speak, was brought into the circle; in the second part the demon was to be identified with the goat; in the third part the two first were joined, and the goat as he died was to repeat the miracle wrought in long ages upon that other victim, by coming to life again humanised by the contact of the ghost of the sorcerer.

It is not permissible to describe the ritual in detail; it is too execrably efficient; but the Turk, brought up in a merciful and cleanly religion, with but few stains of savagery upon it, faltered and nigh fainted and indeed the brains of them all were awhirl. As Eliphas Levi says, evil ceremonies are a true intellectual poison; they do invoke the powers of hallucination and madness as surely as does hashish. And who dare call the phantoms of delirium 'unreal'? They are real enough to kill a man, to ruin a life, to push a soul to every kind of crime; and there are not many 'real' 'material' things that have such weight in work.

Phantoms, then, were apparent to the necromancers; and there was no doubt in any of their minds that they were dealing with actual and malignant entities.

The hideous cries of the tortured cats mingled with the triumphant bleating of the goat and the nasal monotone of Arthwait as he mouthed the words of the *grimoire*. And it seemed to all of them as though the air grew thick and greasy; that of that slime were bred innumerable creeping things, monsters misshapen, abortions of dead paths of evolution, creatures which had not been found fit to live upon the earth and so had been cast off by her as excrement.

It seemed as if the goat were conscious of the phantoms; as if he understood himself as demon king of those regions; for he bounded under the manipulations of Vesquit with such rage and pride that Abdul Bey was forced to use all his strength to hold him. It was taken as a sign of success by all the necromancers; and as Vesquit made the final gesture, Arthwait turned his page, and Abdul struck home with a great knife to the brute's heart.

Now, as the blood stained their grave-clothes, the hearts of the three sorcerers beat heavily. A foul sweat broke out upon them. The sudden change – psychological or magical? – from the turgid drone of Arthwait to the grimness of that silence in which the howls of the agonising cats rose hideous, struck them with a deadly fear. Or was it that they realised for the first time on what a ship they had embarked?

Suppose the corpse did move? Suppose it rose in the power of the devil, and strangled them? Their sweat ran down, and mingled with the blood. The stench of the slain goat was horrible, and the corpse had begun decomposition. The sulphur, burning in little patches here and there, where a candle had fallen and kindled it, added the reek of hell to that of death. Abdul Bey of a sudden was taken deathly sick; at the end he pitched forward, prone upon the corpse. Vesquit pulled him roughly back, and administered a violent stimulant, which made him master of himself.

Now Arthwait started the final conjuration. It can hardly be called language; it was like the jabber of a monkey-house, and like the yells of a thousand savages, and like the moaning of damned souls.

Meanwhile Vesquit proceeded to the last stage of his task. With his knife he hacked off the goat's head, and thrust it into a cavity slashed in the abdomen of the other body. Other parts of the goat he thrust into the mouth of the corpse, while the obscene clamour of the cats mingled with the maniac howls of his colleague.

And then one thing happened which none of them expected. Abdul Bey flung himself down upon the carcasses, and began to tear them with his teeth, and lap the blood with his tongue. Arthwait shrieked out in terror that the Turk had gone mad; but Vesquit understood the truth. Abdul was the most sensitive of the party, and the least developed; it was in him that the spirit of the body, demon-inspired, would manifest.

A few minutes of that scene, and then the Turk sat up. His face expressed the most extreme pleasure. It was the release of a soul from agony that showed itself. But he must have known that his time was short, for he spoke rapidly and earnestly, with febrile energy. And his words were commanding and convincing: Vesquit had no doubt that they were in the presence of knowledge vastly superior to anything that he had yet found.

He wrote down the speech upon the tablets that he had prepared for this purpose.

Hecate will come to help you!

All the powers are at your service; but they are stronger! Treachery shall save you!

Quick! Conceal yourselves awhile. Even so, you are nigh to death!

Oh haste! Look yonder who is standing ready to smite!

The voice dropped. Well was it for Vesquit that he kept his presence of mind. The necromancers looked over their shoulders, and in the east was a blue mist shaped like an egg. In the midst of it, standing upon two crocodiles, was the image of a demon of the underworld, smiling, with his finger upon his lips. Vesquit realised that he was in contact with a force a thousand times greater than any at his disposal. He obeyed instantly the command spoken through Abdul Bey. 'I swear,' he cried, raising his right hand to heaven, 'I swear that we intend you no manner of hurt.' He flushed inwardly, knowing it for a lie, and therefore useless to avert the blow which he felt poised above him. He sought a new form of words. 'I swear that we will not seek to break through your defences.' Abdul Bey gasped out that it was well and fell backwards, as one dead.

In another moment Arthwait, with a yell, a last invocation of that fiend whom he really believed to be omnipotent, entered into spasmodic convulsions, like a man poisoned with strychnine, or dying of tetanus. Vesquit appalled at the fate of his companions, gazed on the figure of the Demon in an agony of fear and horror. It retained the smile, and Vesquit reached his arms towards it. 'Mercy!' he cried, 'oh, my lord, mercy!'

Arthwait was writhing upon the corpses, horribly twisting, foaming black blood from his lungs.

And the old Doctor saw in that instant that his life had been an imbecility, that he had taken the wrong path.

The Demon still smiled. 'Oh my lord!' cried Vesquit, rising to his feet, ' 'twere better I should die.'

The formula of humanity is the willing acceptance of death; and as love, in the male, is itself of the nature of a voluntary death, and therefore a sacrament, so that he who loves slays himself, therefore he who slays himself that life may live becomes a lover. Vesquit stretched out his arms in the sign of the Cross, the symbol of Him who gives life through his own death, or of the instrument of that life and of that death, of the Holy One appointed from the foundation of the world as its redeemer.

It was as if there had come to him a flash of that most

secret Word of all initiated knowledge, so secret and so simple that it may be declared openly in the market-place, and no man hear it. At last he realised himself as a silly old man, whose weakness and pliability in the hands of evil had made him its accomplice. And he saw that death, grasped now, might save him.

The Demon still smiled.

'I invoke the return of the current!' cried Vesquit aloud; and thus, uniting justice with self-sacrifice, he died the death of the righteous.

The image faded away.

The great operation of necromancy had come to naught.

Yet the writing remained; and nearly a day later, when Abdul Bey came to himself, it was the first thing that caught his eye. He thrust it into his shroud, automatically; then stumbled to his feet, and sought his colleagues. At his feet the old Doctor lay dead; Arthwait, his convulsion terminated by exhaustion approximating coma, lay with his head upon the carrion, his tongue lolling from his mouth, chewed to a bloody pulp.

The Turk carried him from the chapel to the villa. His high connections made it easy for him to secure a silent doctor to certify the death of Vesquit, and to attend to Arthwait, who passed from one convulsion to another at frequent intervals. It was almost a month before he could be considered out of danger, and a week after that he was his own man again. The two men then repaired immediately to Paris and vowed never again to speak of, or undertake, another *Experiment in Necromancy.*

AT THE FORK OF THE ROADS

Hypatia Gay knocked timidly at the door of Count Swanoff's flat. Hers was a curious mission, to serve the envy of the long lank melancholy unwashed poet whom she loved. Will Bute was not only a poetaster but a dabbler in magic, and black jealousy of a younger man and a far finer poet gnawed at his petty heart. He had gained a subtle hypnotic influence over Hypatia, who helped him in his ceremonies, and he had now commissioned her to seek out his rival and pick up some magical link through which he might be destroyed.

The door opened, and the girl passed from the cold stone dusk of the stairs to a palace of rose and gold. The poet's rooms were austere in their elegance. A plain gold-black paper of Japan covered the walls; in the midst hung an ancient silver lamp within which glowed the deep ruby of an electric lamp. The floor was covered with black and gold of leopards' skins; on the walls hung a great crucifix in ivory and ebony. Before the blazing fire lay the poet (who had concealed his royal Celtic descent beneath the pseudonym of Swanoff) reading in a great volume bound with vellum.

He rose to greet her.

'Many days have I expected you,' he exclaimed, 'many days have I wept over you. I see your destiny – how thin a thread links you to that mighty Brotherhood of the Silver Star whose trembling neophyte I am – how twisted and thick are the tentacles of the Black Octopus whom you now serve. Ah! wrench yourself away while you are yet linked with us: I would not that you sank into the Ineffable Slime. Blind and bestial are the worms of the Slime: come to me, and by the Faith of the Star, I will save you.'

The girl put him by with a light laugh. 'I came,' she said, 'but to chatter about clairvoyance – why do you threat me with these strange and awful words?'

'Because I see that today may decide all for you. Will you come with me into the White Temple, while I administer the Vows? Or will you enter the Black Temple, and swear away your soul?'

'Oh, really,' she said, 'you are too silly – but I'll do what you like next time I come here.'

'Today your choice – tomorrow your fate,' answered the young poet.

And the conversation drifted to lighter subjects.

But as she left she managed to scratch his hand with a brooch, and this tiny blood-stain on the pin she bore back in triumph to her master; he would work a strange working therewith!

Swanoff closed his books and went to bed. The streets were deadly silent; he turned his thoughts to the Infinite

33

Silence of the Divine Presence, and fell into a peaceful sleep. No dreams disturbed him; later than usual he awoke.

How strange! The healthy flush of his cheek had faded: the hands were white and thin and wrinkled: he was so weak that he could hardly stagger to the bath. Breakfast refreshed him somewhat; but more than this the expectation of a visit from his master.

The master came. 'Little brother!' he cried aloud as he entered, 'you have disobeyed me. You have been meddling again with the Goetia!'

'I swear to you, master!' He did reverence to the adept.

The newcomer was a dark man with a powerful cleanshaven face almost masked in a mass of jet-black hair.

'Little brother,' he said, 'if that be so, then the Goetia has been meddling with you.'

He lifted up his head and sniffed. 'I smell evil,' he said, 'I smell the dark brothers of iniquity. Have you duly performed the Ritual of the Flaming Star?'

'Thrice daily, according to your word.'

'Then evil has entered in a body of flesh. Who has been here?'

The young poet told him. His eyes flashed. 'Aha!' he said, 'now let us Work!'

The neophyte brought writing materials to his master: the quill of a young gander, snow-white; virgin vellum of a young male lamb; ink of the gall of a certain rare fish; and a mysterious Book.

The master drew a number of incomprehensible signs and letters upon the vellum.

'Sleep with this beneath the pillow,' he said: 'you will awake if you are attacked; and whatever it is that attacks you, kill it! Kill it! Kill it! Then instantly go into your temple and assume the shape and dignity of the god Horus; send back the Thing to its sender by the might of the god that is in you! Come! I will discover unto you the words and the signs and the spells for this working of magic art.'

They disappeared into the little white room lined with mirrors which Swanoff used for a temple.

Hypatia Gay, that same afternoon, took some drawings to a publisher in Bond Street. This man was bloated with disease and drink; his loose lips hung in an eternal leer; his fat eyes shed venom; his cheeks seemed ever on the point of bursting into nameless sores and ulcers.

He bought the young girl's drawings. 'Not so much for their value,' he explained, 'as that I like to help promising young artists – like you, my dear!'

Her steely virginal eyes met his fearlessly and unsuspiciously. The beast cowered, and covered his foulness with a hideous smile of shame.

The night came, and young Swanoff went to his rest

without alarm. Yet with that strange wonder that denotes those who expect the unknown and terrible, but have faith to win through.

This night he dreamt – deliciously.

A thousand years he strayed in gardens of spice, by darling streams, beneath delightful trees, in the blue rapture of the wonderful weather. At the end of a long glade of ilex that reached up to a marble palace stood a woman, fairer than all the women of the earth. Imperceptibly they drew together – she was in his arms. He awoke with a start. A woman indeed lay in his arms and showered a rain of burning kisses on his face. She clothed him about with ecstasy; her touch waked the serpent of essential madness in him.

Then, like a flash of lightning, came his master's word to his memory – Kill it! In the dim twilight he could see the lovely face that kissed him with lips of infinite splendour, hear the cooing words of love.

'Kill it! My God! Adonai! Adonai!' He cried aloud, and took her by the throat. Ah God! Her flesh was not the flesh of woman. It was hard as india-rubber to the touch, and his strong young fingers slipped. Also he loved her – loved, as he had never dreamt that love could be.

But he knew now, he knew! And a great loathing mingled with his lust. Long did they struggle; at last he got the upper, and with all his weight above her drove down his fingers in her neck. She gave one gasping cry – a cry of many devils in hell – and died. He was alone.

He had slain the succubus, and absorbed it. Ah! With what force and fire his veins roared! Ah! How he leapt from the bed, and donned the holy robes. How he invoked the God of Vengeance, Horus the mighty, and turned loose the Avengers upon the black soul that had sought his life!

At the end he was calm and happy as a babe; he returned to bed, slept easy, and woke strong and splendid.

Night after night for ten nights this scene was acted and re-acted: always identical. On the eleventh day he received a postcard from Hypatia Gay that she was coming to see him that afternoon.

'It means that the material basis of their working is exhausted,' explained his master. 'She wants another drop of blood. But we must put an end to this.'

They went out into the city, and purchased a certain drug of which the master knew. At the very time that she was calling at the flat, they were at the boarding-house where she lodged, and secretly distributing the drug about the house. Its function was a strange one: hardly had they left the house when from a thousand quarters came a lamentable company of cats, and made the winter hideous with their cries.

'That' (chuckled the master) 'will give her mind something to occupy itself with. She will do no black magic for our friend awhile!'

Indeed the link was broken; Swanoff had peace. 'If she comes again,' ordered the master, 'I leave it to you to punish her.'

A month passed by; then, unannounced, once more Hypatia Gay knocked at the flat. Her virginal eyes still smiled; her purpose was yet deadlier than before.

Swanoff fenced with her awhile. Then she began to tempt him.

'Stay!' he said, 'first you must keep your promise and enter the temple!'

Strong in the trust of her black master, she agreed. The poet opened the little door, and closed it quickly after her, turning the key.

As she passed into the utter darkness that hid behind curtains of black velvet, she caught one glimpse of the presiding god.

It was a skeleton that sat there, and blood stained all its bones. Below it was the evil altar, a round table supported by an ebony figure of a Negro standing upon his hands. Upon the altar smouldered a sickening perfume, and the stench of the slain victims of the god defiled the air. It was a tiny room, and the girl, staggering, came against the skeleton. The bones were not clean; they were hidden by a greasy slime mingling with the blood, as though the hideous worship were about to endow it with a new body of flesh. She wrenched herself back in disgust. Then suddenly she felt it was alive! It was coming towards her! She shrieked once the blasphemy which her vile master had chosen as his mystic name; only a hollow laugh echoed back.

Then she knew all. She knew that to seek the left-hand path may lead one to the power of the blind worms of the Slime – and she resisted. Even then she might have called to the White Brothers; but she did not. A hideous fascination seized her.

And then she felt the horror.

Something – something against which nor clothes nor struggles were any protection – was taking possession of her, eating its way into her . . .

And its embrace was deadly cold . . . Yet the hell-clutch at her heart filled her with a fearful joy. She ran forward; she put her arms round the skeleton; she put her young lips to its bony teeth, and kissed it. Instantly, as at a signal, a drench of the waters of death washed all the human life out of her being, while a rod as of steel smote her even from the base of the spine to the brain. She had passed the gates of the abyss. Shriek after shriek of ineffable agony burst from her tortured mouth; she writhed and howled in that ghastly celebration of the nuptials of the Pit.

Exhaustion took her; she fell with a heavy sob.

When she came to herself she was at home. Still that lamentable crew of cats miauled about the house. She awoke and shuddered. On the table lay two notes.

The first: 'You fool! They are after me; my life is not safe. You have ruined me – Curse you!' This from the loved master, for whom she had sacrificed her soul.

The second a polite note from the publisher, asking for more drawings. Dazed and desperate, she picked up her portfolio, and went round to his office in Bond Street.

He saw the leprous light of utter degradation in her eyes; a dull flush came to his face; he licked his lips.

THE BLACK LODGE

✳

The Operation planned by the Black Lodge was simple and colossal both in theory and in practice. It was based on the prime principle of Sympathetic Magic, which is that if you destroy anything which is bound up with anybody by an identifying link that person also perishes. Douglas had adroitly taken advantage of the fact of the analogy between his own domestic situation and that of Cyril Grey. He had no need to attack the young magician directly, or even his wife, Lisa; he had merely to conduct the required ritual and this would undoubtedly bring about the downfall of his enemy. For if he could bring Cyril's magic to naught, that exorcist would be destroyed by the recoil of his own exorcism. The laws of force take no account of human prejudices about 'good' or 'evil'; if one is run over by a railway engine, it matters nothing, physically, whether one is trying to commit suicide or to save a child. The difference in the result lies wholly on a superior plane.

For great operations – the 'set pieces' of his diabolical pyrotechnics – Douglas had a place set apart and prepared. This was an old wine-cellar in a street between the Seine and the Boulevard St Germain. The entrance was comparatively reputable, being a house of cheap prostitution which he and one of his associates, Balloch – screened behind a woman – owned between them. Below this house was a cellar where the apaches of Paris gathered to dance and plot against society; so ran the legend, and two burly *sergents de ville*, with fixed bayonets and cocked revolvers lying on the table before them, superintended the revels. For in fact Douglas had perceived that the apache spent no money, and that it would pay better to run the cellar as a show place for Americans, Englishmen, Germans, and country cousins from the provinces on a jaunt to Paris, on the hunt for thrills. No one more dangerous than a greengrocer had crossed that threshold for many a long year, and the visible apaches, drinking and swearing, dancing an alleged can-can and occasionally throwing bottles and knives to each other, were honest folk painfully earning the exiguous salary which the 'long firm' paid them.

But beneath this cellar, unknown even to the police, was a vault which had once served for storing spirits. It was below the level of the river; rats, damp, and stale alcohol gave it an atmosphere happily peculiar to such abodes. There is no place in the world more law-abiding than a house of ill-fame, with the light of police supervision constantly upon it; and the astuteness of the sorcerer in choosing this for his place of evocation was rewarded by complete freedom from disturbance or suspicion. Anyone could enter at any hour of day or night, with every precaution of secrecy, without drawing more than a laugh from the police on guard.

The entrance to the sorcerer's den was similarly concealed – by cunning, not by more obvious methods.

A sort of cupboard-shelf, reached by a ladder from the dancing cellar and by a few steps from one of the bedrooms in the house above, was called 'Troppman's refuge', it being said that that celebrated murderer once had lain concealed there for some days. His autograph, and some bad verses (all contributed by an ingenious cabaret singer) were shown upon the walls. It was therefore quite natural and unsuspicious for any visitor to climb up into that room, which was so small that it would only hold one man of average size. His non-appearance would not cause surprise; he might have gone out the other way; in fact, he would naturally do so. But in the moment of his finding himself alone, he could, if he knew the secret, press a hidden lever which caused the floor to descend bodily. Arrived below, a corridor with three right-angled turns – this could, incidentally, be flooded at need in a few moments – led to the last of the defences, a regular door such as is fitted to a strong-room. There was an emergency exit to the cellar, equally ingenious; it was a sort of torpedo-tube opening beneath the water of the Seine. It was fitted with a compressed air-chamber. Anyone wishing to escape had merely to introduce himself into a shell made of thin cork, and shoot into the river. Even the worst of swimmers could be sure to reach the neighbouring quay. But the secret of this was known only to Douglas and one other.

The very earliest steps in such thoroughgoing sorcery as Douglas practised require the student to deform and mutilate his humanity by accustoming himself to such moral crimes as render their perpetrator callous and insensible to all such emotions as men naturally cherish; in particular, love. The Black Lodge put all its members through regular practices of cruelty and meanness. Guy de Maupassant wrote two of the most revolting stories ever told; one of a boy who hated a horse, the other of a family of peasants who tortured a blind relative that had been left to their charity. Such vileness as is written there by the divine hand of that great artist forbids emulation; the reverent reference must suffice.

Enough to say that stifling of all natural impulse was a preliminary of the system of the Black Lodge; in higher grades the pupil took on the manipulation of subtler forces. Douglas's own use of his wife's love to vitriolise her heart was considered by the best judges as likely to become a classic.

The inner circle, the fourteen men about Douglas himself and that still more mysterious person to whom even he was responsible, a woman known only as 'Annie' or as 'A.B.', were sealed to him by the direst of all bonds. Needless are oaths in the Black Lodge; honour being the first thing discarded, their only use is to frighten fools. But before joining the Fourteen, known as the Ghaaghaael, it was obligatory to commit a murder in cold blood, and to place the proofs of it in the hands of Douglas. Thus each step in sorcery is also a step in slavery; and that any man should put such power in the hands of another, no matter for what hope of gain, is one of the mysteries of perverse psychology. The highest rank in the Lodge was called Thaumiel-Qeretiel, and there were two of these, 'Annie' and Douglas, who were alone in possession of the full secrets of the Lodge. Only they and the Fourteen had keys to the cellar and the secret of the combination.

Beginners were initiated there, and the method of introducing them was satisfactory and ingenious. They were taken to the house in an automobile, their eyes blinded by an ordinary pair of motor-goggles, behind whose glass was a steel plate.

The cellar itself was arranged as a permanent place of evocation. It was a far more complex device than that used by Vesquit in Naples, for in confusion lay the safety of the Lodge. The floor was covered with symbols which even the Fourteen did not wholly understand; any one of them, crossed inadvertently, might be a magical trap for a traitor; and as each of the Fourteen was exactly that, in fact had to be so to qualify for supreme place, it was with abject fear that this Unholy of Unholies was guarded.

At the appointed hour the Fourteen assembled at the Beth Chol, or House of Horror, as the cellar was called in the jargon of the sorcerers. Among their number were the aforementioned Balloch; Cremers, a priest from America; Abdul Bey, a Turk, and Douglas's wife.

The first part of the procedure consisted in the formal renunciation by Mrs Douglas of the vows taken for her in her baptism, a ceremonial apostacy from Christianity. This was done in no spirit of hostility to that religion, but to permit of her being rebaptised into it under Lisa's maiden name. The Turk was next called upon to renounce Islam, and baptised by the name of the Marchese la Giuffria.

The American priest next proceeded to confirm them in the Christian religion, and to communicate the Sacrament.

Finally, they were married. In this long profanation of the mysteries of the Church the horror lay in the business-like simplicity of the procedure.

One can imagine the Charity of a devout Christian finding excuses for the Black Mass, when it is the expression of the revolt of an agonising soul, or of the hysteria of a half-crazed debauchee; he can conceive of repentance and of grace following upon enlightenment; but this cold-blooded abuse of the most sacred rites, their quite casual employment as the mere prelude to a crime which is tantamount to murder in the opinion of all right-minded men, must seem even to the freethinker or the Pagan as an abomination not to be forgiven.

No pains had been spared by Douglas to make all secure. Balloch and Cremers had sponsored both 'infants', and Douglas himself, as having most right, gave his wife in marriage to the Turk.

A brutally realistic touch was needed to consumate the sacrilege; it was not neglected.

Much of the pleasure taken by Douglas in this miserable and criminal farce was due to his enjoyment of the sufferings of his wife. Each new spurt of filth wrung her heart afresh; and withal she was aware that all these things were but the prelude to an act of fiendish violence more horrible than them all.

Then Cremers and Abdul Bey, their functions ended, were led out of the cellar. Balloch remained to perform the operation from which the bulk of his income was derived.

But there was yet much sorcery of the more secret sort to be accomplished. Douglas who, up to now, had confined himself to intense mental concentration upon the work, forcing himself to believe that the ceremonies he was witnessing were real instead of mockery, that his wife was really Lisa, and Abdul really the Marchese, now came forward as the heart and brain of the work. The difficulty – the crux of the whole art – had been to introduce Cyril Grey into the affair, and this had been overcome by the use of a specimen of his signature. But now it was necessary also to dedicate the victim to Hecate, or rather, to her Hebrew equivalent, Nahema, the devourer of little children, because she also is one aspect of the moon, and Lisa having been adopted to that planet, her representative must needs undergo a similar ensorcelment.

In the art of evocation Douglas was profoundly skilled. His mind was of a material and practical order, and distrusted subtleties. He gladly endured the immense labour of compelling a spirit to visible appearance, when a less careful or more fine-minded sorcerer would have worked upon some other plane. He had so far mastered his art that in a place, such as he now had, long habitated to similar scenes, he could call up a visible image of almost any demon required in a period of not more than half an hour. For place-association is of great importance, possibly because it favours concentration of mind. Evidently, it is difficult not to feel religious in King's College Chapel, Cambridge, or otherwise than profoundly sceptical and Pagan in St Peter's, at Rome, with its 'East' in the West, its adaptation of a statue of Jupiter to represent its patron saint, and the emphasis of its entire architecture in bearing witness that its true name is Temporal Power. Gothic is the only mystic type;

Templar and Byzantine are only religious through sexuality; Perpendicular is more moral than spiritual – and modern architecture means nothing at all.

In the Beth Chol there was always a bowl of fresh bull's blood burning over a charcoal brazier.

Science is gradually being forced round once more to the belief that there is something more in life than its mere chemistry and physics. Those who practise the occult arts have never been in doubt on the subject. The dynamic virtue of living substance does not depart from it immediately at death. Those ideas, therefore, which seek manifestation in life, must do so either by incarnation or by seizing some still living matter which the idea or soul in possession has abandoned. Sorcerers consequently employ the fumes of fresh blood as a vehicle for the manifestation of the demons whom they wish to evoke. The matter is easy enough; for fiends are always eager to take hold on the sensory life. Occasionally, such beings find people ignorant and foolish enough to offer themselves deliberately to obsession by sitting in a dark room without magical protection, and inviting any wandering ghost or demon to take hold of them, and use their bodies and minds. This loathsome folly is called Spiritualism, and successful practitioners can be recognised by the fact that their minds are no use for anything at all any more. They become incapable of mental concentration, or a connected train of thought; only too often the obsessing spirit gains power to take hold of them at will, and utters by their mouths foulness and imbecility when the whim takes him. True souls would never seek so ignoble a means of manifesting in earth-life; their ways are holy, and in accord with Nature.

While the true soul reincarnates as a renunciation, a sacrifice of its divine life and ecstasy for the sake of redeeming those who are not yet freed from mortal longings, the demon seeks incarnation as a means of gratifying unslaked lusts.

Like a dumb beast in pain, the wife of Douglas watched her husband go through his ghastly ritual, with averted face, as is prescribed; for none may look on Hecate, and remain sane. The proper conjurations of Hecate are curses against all renewal of life; her sacrament is deadly night-shade or henbane, and her due offering a black lamb torn ere its birth from a black ewe.

This, with sardonic subter-thought, pleasing to Hecate, the sorcerer promised her as she made her presence felt; whether they could have seen anything if they had dared to look, who can say? But through the cellar moved an icy sensation, as if some presence had indeed been called forth by the words and rites spoken and accomplished.

For Hecate is what Scripture calls 'the second death'. Natural death is to man the greatest of the Sacrements, of which all others are but symbols; for it is the final and absolute Union with the creator, and it is also the Pylon of the Temple of Life, even in the material world, for Death is Love.

Certainly the wife of Douglas felt the presence of that vile thing evoked from Tartarus. Its chill struck through to her bones. Nothing had so torn her breast as the constant refusal of her husband to allow her to fulfil her human destiny. Even her prostitution, since it was forced upon her by the one man she loved, might be endured – if only – if only –

But always the aid of Balloch had been summoned; always, in dire distress, and direr danger, she had been thwarted of her life's purpose. It was not so much a conscious wish, though that was strong, as an actual physical craving of her nature, as urgent and devouring as hunger or thirst.

Balloch, who had been all his life high-priest of Hecate, had never been present at an evocation of the force that he served. He shuddered – not a little – as the sorcerer recited his surgical exploits; the credentials of the faith of her servant then present before her. He had committed his dastardly crimes wholly for gain, and as a handle for blackmail; the magical significance of the business had not occurred to him at all. His magical work had been almost entirely directed to the gratification of sensuality in abnormal and extra-human channels. So, while a fierce pride now thrilled him, there was mingled with it a sinking of the spirit; for he realised that its mistress had been sterility and death. And it was of death that he was most afraid. The cynical calm of Douglas appalled him; he recognised the superiority of that great sorcerer; and his hope to supplant him died within his breast.

At that moment Hecate herself passed into him, and twined herself inextricably about his brain. He accepted his destiny as her high-priest; in future he would do murder for the joy of pleasing her! All other mistresses were tame to this one! The thrill of Thuggee caught him – and in a very spasm of maniacal exaltation, he vowed himself again and again to her services. She should be sole goddess of the Black Lodge – only let her show him how to get rid of Douglas! Instantly the plan came to him; he remembered that 'Annie' was high-priestess of Hecate in a greater sense than himself; for she was notorious as an open advocate of this kind of murder; indeed, she had narrowly escaped prison on this charge; he would tempt Douglas to rid himself of 'Annie' – and then betray him to her.

So powerful was the emotion that consumed him that he trembled with excitement and eagerness. Tonight was a great night: it was a step in his initiation to take part in so tremendous a ceremony. He became nervously exalted; he could have danced; Hecate, warming herself in his old bones, communicated a devilish glee to him.

The moment was at hand for his renewed activity.

'Hecate, mother only of death, devourer of all life!' cried Douglas, in his final adjuration; 'as I devote to thy chill tooth this secret spring of man, so be it with all that are like unto it! Even as it is with that which I shall cast upon thine altar, so be it with all the offspring of Lisa la Guiffria!'

He ended with the thirteenth repetition of that appalling curse which begins 'ΕΙΙΙΚΑΟΜΑΙ ΚΕ ΤΗΝ ΕΝ ΤΩΙ ΚΕΝΕΩΙ, ΙΙΝΕΨΜΑΤΙ, ΓΕΙΝΑΝ, ΑΟΡΑΤΑΝ, ΙΙΑΝΤΟΚΡΑΤΟΡΑ, ΕΡΟΙΙΟΙΑΝ ΚΑΙ ΕΡΗΜΟΙΙΟΙΑΝ, 'ΗΜΙΚΟΝΤΑ 'ΟΚΙΑΝ 'ΕΚΤΑΟΚΑΝ calling upon 'her that dwelleth in the void place, the inane, terrible, inexorable, maker of horror and desolation, hater of the house that prospereth', and devoting 'the signified and sealed, named and unnamed' to destruction.

Then he turned to Balloch, and bade him act. Three minutes later the surgeon gave a curse, and blanched, as a scream, despite herself, burst from the bitten lips of the brave woman who lay upon the altar.

'Why couldn't you let me give an anaesthetic?' he said angrily.

'What's wrong? Is it bad?'

'It's damned ugly. Curse it; not a thing here that I need!'

But he needed nothing; he had done more even than he guessed.

Mrs Douglas, her face suddenly drawn and white, lifted her head with infinite effort towards her husband.

'I've always loved you,' she whispered, 'and I love you now, as – I – die.'

Her head dropped with a dull crack upon the slab. No one can say if she heard the reply of Douglas:

'You sow! you've bitched the whole show!'

For she had uttered the surepeme name of Love, in love; and the spell dissolved more swiftly than a dream. There was no Hecate, no sorcerer even, for the moment; nothing but two murderers, and the corpse of a martyr between them.

Douglas did not waste a single word of abuse on Balloch.

'This is for you to clear up,' he said, with a simplicity that cut deeper than sneer or snarl, and walked out of the cellar.

Balloch, left to himself, became hysterical. In his act he recognised the first-fruits of the divine possession; his offering to the goddess had been stupendous indeed. All his exaltation returned: now would Hecate favour him above all men!

THE DREAM CIRCEAN

I

Perched at the junction of two of the steepest little streets in Montmartre shines the 'Lapin Agile,' a tiny window filled with gleaming bottles, thrilled through by the light behind, a little terrace with tables, chairs and shrubs, and two dark doors.

Roderic Mason came striding up the steepness of the Rue St. Vincent, his pipe gripped hard in his jaw; for the hill is too abrupt for lounging. On the terrace he stretched himself, twirled round half a dozen times like a dervish, pocketed his pipe, and went stooping through the open doorway.

Grand old Frédéric was there, in his vast corduroys and sou'wester hat, a 'cello in his hand.

His trim grey beard was a shade whiter than when Roderic had last patronized the 'Lapin,' five years before; but the kindly, gay, triumphant eyes were nowise dimmed by time. He knew Roderic at a glance, and gave his left hand carelessly, as if he had been gone but yesterday. Time ambles easily for the owner of such an eyrie, his life content with wine and song and simple happiness.

It is in such as Frédéric that the hope of the world lies. You could not bribe Frédéric with a motor-car to grind in an office and help to starve and enslave his fellows. The bloated, short-of-breath, bedizened magnates of commerce and finance are not life, but a disease. The monster hotel is not hospitality, but imprisonment. Civilization is a madness; and while there are men like Frédéric there is a hope that it will pass. Woe to the earth when Bumble and Rockefeller and their victims are the sole economic types of man!

Roderic sat down on his favourite bench against the wall, and took stock of things.

How well he remembered the immense Christ at the end of the room, a figure conceived by a giant of old time, one might have thought, and now covered with a dry, green lichenous rot, so that the limbs were swollen and distorted. It gave an incredibly strong impression of loathsome disease, entirely overpowering the intention of picturing inflicted pain.

Roderic, who, far from being a good man, was actually a Freethinker, thought it a grimly apt symbol of the religion of our day.

On His right stood a plaster Muse, with a lvre, the effect being decidedly improved by someone who had affixed a comic mask with a grinning mouth and a long pink nose; on His left a stone plaque of Lakshmi, the Hindu Venus, a really very fine piece of work, clean and dignified, in a way the one sanity in the room, except for an exquisite pencil sketch of a child, done with all the delicacy and strength of

Whistler. The rest of the decoration was a delicious mixture of the grotesque and the obscene. Sketches, pastels, cuts, cartoons, oils, all the media of art, had been exhausted in a noble attempt to flagellate impurity—impurity of thought, line, colour, all we symbolize by womanhood.

Hence the grotesque obscenity in nowise suggested Jewry; but gave a wholesome reaction of life and youth against artificiality and money-lust.

As it chanced, there was nobody of importance in the 'Lapin.' Frédéric, with his hearty voice and his virile roll, more of a dance than a walk, easily dominated the company.

Yet there was at least one really remarkable figure in the pleasant gloom of the little cabaret.

A man sat there, timid, pathetic, one would say a man often rebuffed. He was nigh seventy years of age, maybe; he looked older. For him time had not moved at all, apparently; for he wore the dress of a beau of the Second Empire.

Exquisitely, too, he wore it. Sitting back in his dark corner, the figure would have gained had it been suddenly transplanted to the glare of a state ball and the steps of a throne.

Merrily Frédéric trolled out an easy, simple song with the perfect art—how different from the laborious inefficiency of the Opera!—and came over to Roderic to see that his coffee was to his liking.

'Changes, Frédéric,!' he said, a little sadly. 'Where is Madeleine la Vache?'

'At Lourcine.'

'Mimi l'Engeuleuse?'

'At Clamart.'

'The Scotch Count, who always spoke like a hanging judge?'

'Went to Scotland—he could get no more whisky here on credit.'

'His wife?'

'Poor girl! poor girl!'

'Ah! it was bound to happen. And Bubu Tire-Cravat?'

Frédéric brought the edge of his hand down smartly on the table, with a laugh.

'He had made so many widows, it was only fair he should marry one!' commented the Englishman. And Pea-shooter Charley?'

'Don't know. I think he is in prison in England.'

'Well, well; it saddens. "Where are the snows of yesteryear?" I must have an absinthe; I feel old.'

'You are half my years,' answered Frédéric. 'But come! If yesteryear be past, it is this year now. And all these distinguished persons who are gone, together are not worth one silver shoe-buckle of yonder—' Frédéric nodded towards the old beau.

'True, I never knew him; yet he looks as if he had sat there since Sedan. Who is he?'

'We do not know his name, monsieur,' said Frédéric softly, a little awed; 'but I think he was a duke, a prince—I cannot say what. He is more than that—he is unique. He is—*le Revenant de la Rue des Quatre Vents*!'

'The Ghost of the Street of the Four Winds,' Roderic was immensely taken by the title; a thousand fantastic bases for the sobriquet jumped into his brain. Was the Rue des Quatre Vents haunted by a ghost in his image? There are no ghosts in practical Paris. But of all the ideas which came to him, not one was half so strange as the simple and natural story which he was later to hear.

'Come,' said Frédéric. 'I will present you to him.'

'Monseigneur,' he said, as Roderic stood before him, ready to make his little bow, let me present Monsieur Mason, an Englishman.'

The old fellow took no notice. Said Frédéric in his ear: 'Monsieur lives on the Boulevard St. Germain, and loves to paint the streets.'

The old man rose with alacrity, smiled, bowed, was enchanted to meet one of the gallant allies whose courage had—he spoke glibly of the Alma, Inkerman, Sebastopol.

The little comedy had not been lost on Roderic. Wondering, he sat down beside the old nobleman.

What spell had Frédéric wrought of so potent a complexion?

'Sir,' he said, 'the gallantry of the French troops at the Malakoff was beyond all praise; it will live for ever in history.'

To another he might have spoken of the *entente cordiale;* to this man he dared not.

Had not his brain perhaps stopped in the sixties?

Had the catastrophe of '70 broken his heart?

Roderic must walk warily.

But the conversation did not take the expected turn. The old gentleman elegantly, wittily, almost gaily, chattered of art, of music, of the changed appearance of Paris. Here, at any rate, he was *au courant des affaires.*

Yet as Roderic, puzzled and pleased, finished his absinthe he said more seriously than he had yet spoken: 'I hear that monsieur is a great painter' (Roderic modestly waved aside the adjective), 'has painted many pictures of Paris. Indeed, as I think of it, I seem to remember a large picture of St. Sulpice at the Salon of eight years ago—no, seven years ago.'

Roderic stared in surprise. How should any one—such a man, of all men—remember his daub, a thing he himself had long forgotten? The oldster read his thought. 'There was one corner of that picture which interested me deeply, deeply,' he said. 'I called to see you; you had gone—none knew where.

I am indeed glad to have met you at last. Perhaps you would be good enough to show me your pictures—you have other pictures of Paris? I am interested in Paris—in Paris itself—in the stones and bricks of it. Might I—if you have nothing better to do—come to your studio now, and see them?'

'I'm afraid the light—' began Roderic. It was now ten o'clock.

'That is nothing,' returned the other. 'I have my own criteria of excellence. A match-glimmer serves me.'

There was only one explanation of all this. The man must be an architect, perhaps ruined in the mad speculations of the Empire, so well described by Zola in *La Curée*.

'At your service, sir,' he said, and rose. The old fellow was surely eccentric; but equally he was not dangerous. He was rich, or he would not be wearing a diamond worth every penny of two thousand pounds, as Roderic, no bad judge, made out. There might be profit, and there would assuredly be pleasure.

They waved, the one an airy, the other a courteous, goodnight to grand old Frédéric, and went out.

The old man was nimble as a kitten; he had all the suppleness of youth; and together they ran rapidly down to the boulevard, where, hailing a fiacre, they jumped in and clattered down towards the Seine.

Roderic sat well back in the carriage, a little lost in thought.

But the old man sat upright, and peered eagerly about him. Once he stopped the cab suddenly at a house with a low railing in front of it, well set back from the street, jumped out, examined it minutely, and then, with a sigh and a shake of the head, came back, a little wearier, a little older.

They crossed the Seine, rattled up the Rue Bonaparte, and stopped at the door of Roderic's studio.

II

'Ah, well, said the old man, as he concluded his examination of the pictures, 'What I seek is not here. If it will not weary you, I will tell you a story. Perhaps, although you have not painted it, you have seen it. Perhaps—bah! I am seventy years of age, and a fool to the end.

'Listen, my young friend! I was not always seventy years of age, and that of which I have to tell you happened when I was twenty-two.

'In those days I was very rich, and very happy. I had never loved; I cared for nobody. My parents were both dead long since. A year of freedom from the control of my good old guardian, the Duc de Castelnaudary (God rest his soul!), had left me yet taintless as a flower. I had that chivalrous devotion to woman which perhaps never really existed at any time save for rare individuals.

'Such a one is ripe for adventure, and since, as your great

poet has said, "Circumstance bows before those who never miss a chance," it was perhaps only a matter of time before I met with one.

'Indeed (I will tell you, for it will help you to understand my story), I once found myself in an extremely absurd position through my fantastic trust in the impeccability of woman.

'It was rather late one night, and I was walking home through a deserted street, when two brutal-looking ruffians came towards me, between them a young and beautiful girl, her face flushed with shame, and screaming in pain; for the savages had each firm hold of one arm, and were forcing her at a rapid pace—to what vile den?

'My fist in the face of one and my foot in the stomach of the other! They sprawled in the road, and, disdaining them, I turned my back and offered my arm to the girl. She, in an excess of gratitude, flung her arms round my neck and began to kiss me furiously—the first kiss I had ever had from a woman, mind you! Maybe I would not have been altogether displeased, but that she stank so foully of brandy that—my gorge rises at the memory. The ruffians, more surprised than hurt, began laughing, but kept well away. I tried to induce the girl to come home; in the end she lost her temper, and fell to belabouring me with her fists. I was not strong enough or experienced enough to contend with a madwoman, and I could not allow myself to strike her. She beat me sore. . . .

'I can remember the scene now as if it were yesterday: the bewildered boy, the screaming, swearing, kicking, scratching woman, the two "savages" (honest *bourgeois* enough!) reeling against the houses, crying with laughter, too weak with laughter to stand straight.

'By-and-by they took pity, came forward, and released me from the unpleasant situation.

'But the shame of me, as I slunk away down the streets! I would not go home that night at all, ashamed to face my own servants.

'I told myself, in the end, that this was a rare accident; but for all that there must have remained a slight stain upon the mirror of perfect chivalry. In the old days when they taught logic in the schools one learnt how delicate a flower was a "universal affirmative."

'It was some uneventful months after this "tragedy of the ideal" that I was again walking home very late. I had been to the Jardin des Plantes in the afternoon, and, dining in that quarter, had stayed lingering on the bridge watching the Seine. The moon dropped down behind the houses—with a start I realized that I must go home. There was some danger, you understand, of footpads. Nothing, however, occurred until—I always preferred to walk through the narrow streets; there is romance in narrow streets!—I found myself in the

Rue des Quatre Vents; not a stone's-throw from this house, as you know.

'I had been thinking of my previous misadventure, and, with the folly of youth, had been indulging in a reverie of the kind that begins "If only." If only she had been a princess ravished by a wicked ogre. If only . . . If only . . .

'On the south side of the Rue des Quatre Vents is a house standing well back from the street, with a railing in front of it—a common type, is it not? But what riveted my attention upon it was that while the front of the house was otherwise entirely dark, from a window on the first floor streamed a blaze of light. The window was wide open to the street; voices came from it.

'The first an old, harsh, menacing voice, with all the sting of hate in it; nay, the sting of something devilish, worse than hate. A corrupt enjoyment of its malice informed it. And the words it spoke were too infamous for me to repeat. They are scarred upon my brain. Addressed to the vilest harridan that scours the gutter for her carrion prey, they would have yet been inhuman, impossible; to the voice that answered . . . !

'It was a voice like the tinkling of a fairy bell. Whoever spoke was little more than a child; and her answer had the purity and strength of an angel. That even the foul monster who addressed her could support it, unblasted, was matter for astonishment.

'Now the older voice broke into filthy insult, a very frenzy of malice.

'I heard—O God!—the swish of a whip, and the sound of it falling upon flesh.

'There was silence, awhile, save for the hideous laughter of the invisible horror inside.

'At last a piteous little moan.

'My blood sang shrill within me. Out of myself, I sprang at the railings, and was over them in a second. Rapidly, and quite unobserved (for the scene was strenuous within), I climbed up the grating of the lower windows, and, reaching up to the edge of the balcony, swung myself up to and over it.

'As I stopped to fetch breath, as yet unperceived, I took in the scene, and was staggered at its strangeness.

'The room, though exquisitely decorated, was entirely bare of furniture, unless one could dignify by that name a heap of dirty straw in one corner, by which stood a flattish wooden bowl, half full of what looked like a crust of bread mashed into pulp with water.

'Half turned away from me stood the owner of the harsh voice and soul abominable. It was a woman of perhaps sixty years of age, the head of an angel—so regular were the features, so silver-white the hair—set upon the deformed body of a dwarf. Hairy hands and twisted arms, a hunched back and bandy legs; in the gnarled right hand a terrible whip, the carved jade handle blossoming into a rose of fine cords, shining with silver—sharp, three-cornered chips of silver! The whole dripped black with blood. Upon the angel face stood a sneer, a snarl, a malediction. The effect upon one's sense of something beyond the ordinary was, too, heightened by her costume; for though the summer was at its height she was clad from head to foot in ermine, starred, more heavily than is usual, with the little black tails in the form of *fleurs-de-lis*.

'In extreme contrast to this monster was a young girl crouching upon the floor. At first sight one would have hardly suspected a human form at all, for from her head flowed down on all sides a torrent of exquisite blonde gold, that completely hid her. Only two little hands looked out, clasped, pleading for mercy, and a fairy child-face looking up—in vain—to that black heart of hatred. Even as I gazed the woman hissed out so frightful a menace that my blood ran chill. The child shrank back into herself. The other raised her whip. I leapt into the room. The old hag spat one infamous word at me, turned on me with the whip.

'This time I was under no illusions about the sanctity of womanhood. With a single blow I felled her to the ground. My signet-ring cut her lip, and the blood trickled over her cheek. I laughed. But the child never moved—it would seem she hardly comprehended.

'I turned, bowed. "I could not bear to hear your cries," I said—rather obviously, one may admit. "I came—" adding under my breath, "I saw, I conquered." "Who is that?" I added sternly, pointing to the prostrate hag.

' "Ah, sir" (she began to cry), "it is my mother." The horror of it was tenfold multiplied. "She—she—" The child blushed, stammered, stopped.

' "I heard, mademoiselle," I cried indignantly.

' "I am here" (she sobbed) "for a month, starved, whipped—oh! By day the window barred with iron; by night, open, the more to mock my helplessness!" Then, with a sudden cry, her little pink hand darting out and showing a faultless arm: "Look! look! she is on you."

'The mother had drawn herself away with infinite stealth, regained her feet, and, a thin stiletto in her hand, was crouched to spring. Indeed, as she leapt I was hard put to it to avoid the lunge; the dagger-edge grazed my arm as I stepped aside.

'I turned. She was on me, flinging me aside with the force of her rush as if I had been a straw. The snarl of her was like a wolf.

'This time she cut me deep. Again a whirl, a rush. I altered my tactics; I ran in to meet her. Hampered as she was by her furs, I was now quicker than she. I struck her dagger arm so strongly that the blade flew into the air, and fell quivering on the floor, the heavy hilt driving the thin blade deep into the polished wood. Even so I had her by the waist, catching her arm, and with one heave of my back I tossed her into the air, careless where she might fall.

'As luck would have it, she struck the balcony rail, broke it, and fell upon the pavement of the court. There was a crash, but no cry, no groan. I went to the balcony. She lay still, as the living do not lie, and her white hair was blackening, lapped by a congealing stream.

'I withdrew into the room. Since I have learnt that any death brings with it a strange sense of relief. There is a certain finality. *La comédie est jouée*—and one turns with new life to the next business.

'The golden child had never stirred. But now she crouched lower, and fell to soft, sweet crying.

' "Your mother is dead," I said abruptly. "May I offer you the guardianship of my godmother, the Duchess of Castelnaudary? Come, mademoiselle, let us go."

' "I thank you, sir," she answered, still sobbing; "but Jean is awake and at the door. Jean is fierce and lean as an old wolf."

'I pulled the dagger from the floor. "I am fierce and lithe as a young lion!" I said. "Let the old wolf beware!"

' "But I cannot, sir, I cannot. I. . . ." Her confusion became acute.

' "I dare not move, sir—I—I—my mother has taken away all my clothes."

'I marvelled. In her palace of gold hair nobody could have guessed it. But now I blushed, and lively. The dilemma was absurd.

' "I have it," said I. "I will climb down and bring up the ermine."

'She shuddered at the idea. Her dead mother's furs!

' "It must be," I said firmly.

' "Go, brave knight!'—a delicate smile lit up her face—"I trust myself to you."

'I bent on my right knee to her. "I take you," I said, "to be my lady, to fight in your cause, to honour and love you for ever."

'She put out her right hand—oh, the delicate beauty of it! I kissed it. "My knight," she said, "Jean is below; he may hear you; you go perhaps to your death—kiss me!"

'With a sob I sought her once full in my arms, and our mouths met. I closed my eyes in trance; my muscles failed; I sank, my forehead to the ground before her.

'When I opened my eyes again she too was praying. Softly, without a word, I stepped to the window, took the dagger in my teeth, dropped from the edge, landed lightly beside the corpse. She was quite dead, the skull broken in, the teeth exposed in a last snarl. She lay on her back; I opened the coat, turned her over. The gruesome task was nearly finished when the door of the house opened, and an old man, his face scarred, one lip cut half away in some old brawl, so that he grinned horribly and askew, rushed out at me, a rapier in his hand. My stiletto, though long beyond the ordinary, was useless against a tool of such superior reach.

'A last wrench gave me the ermine cloak, an invaluable parry. Could I entangle his sword, he was at my mercy. He saw it, and fenced warily. Indeed, I had the upper hand throughout. Threatening to throw the cloak, catch his sword, blind him, rush in with my dagger—he gave back and back in a circle round the courtyard.

'No sound came from the room above. Probably we three were alone. The fight was not to be prolonged for ever; the weight of the fur would tire me soon, counter-balance the advantage of age. Then, almost before I knew what had happened, we were fighting in the street. I would not cry for help; one was more likely to rouse a bandit than a guardian of the peace. And, besides, who could say how the law stood?

'I had certainly killed a lady; I was doing my best, with the aid of her stolen cloak, to kill a servant of the house; I contemplated an abduction. Best kill him silently, and be gone.

'But when and how had Jean pulled open the iron gates

and retreated into the street?

'It mattered little, though certainly it left an uneasy sense of bewilderment; what mattered was that here we were fighting in semi-darkness—the dawn was not fairly lifted—for life and death.

' "Ten thousand crowns, Monsieur Jean," I cried, "and my service!"—I gave him my style—"I see you can be a faithful servant."

' "Faithful to death!" he retorted, and I was sorry to have to kill him.

'We fenced grimly on.

' "But," I urged, "your mistress is dead. Your duty is to her child, and I am her child's—"

'He looked up from my eyes. "An omen!" he cried, pointing to the great statue of St. Michael trampling Satan, for we had come fighting to the Place St. Michel. "Darkness yields to light; I am your servant, sir." He dropped on one knee, and tendered the hilt of his sword.

'But as I put out my hand to take it (guarded against attack, I boast me, but not against the extraordinary trick which followed) he suddenly snatched at the ermine, which lay loosely on my left arm, and, leaving me with sword and dagger, fled with a shriek of laughter across the Place St. Michel, and, flinging the furs over the bridge, himself plunged into the Seine and swam strongly for the other bank.

There was no object in pursuing him; I would recover the furs, and return triumphant. Alas! they had sunk; they were now whirled far away by the swift river. Where should I get a cloak?

'How stupid of me! The old woman had plenty of other clothes beneath her furs; I would take them.

'And I set myself gaily to run back to the house.

III

'Whether by excitement I took the wrong turning, or whether—but you will hear!—in short, I do not clearly understand even now why I did not at once find the road. But at least I did fail to find it, discovered, as I supposed, my error, corrected it, failed once more. . . . In the end I got flustered—so much hung on my speedy return!—I fluttered hither and thither like a wild pigeon whose mate has been shot. I stopped short, pulled myself together. Let me think it out! Where am I now? I was under the shadow (the dawn just lit its edge) of the mighty shoulder of St., Sulpice. "More haste, less speed!" I said to myself. "I will walk deliberately down to the boulevard, turn east, and so I cannot possibly miss the Carrefour de l'Odéon"—out of which, as I knew of old, the Rue des Quatre Vents leads. Indeed, I remembered the carrefour from that night. I had passed through it. I remembered hesitating as to which turning to take. For, as you know, the carrefour is a triangle, one road leading from the apex, four (with two minor variations just off the carrefour) from the base.

'Following this plan, I came, sure enough, in three minutes or so into the Rue des Quatre Vents. It is not a long street, as you know, and I thought that I remembered perfectly that the house faced the tiny Rue St. Grégoire, which leads back to the Boulevard St. Germain. Indeed, it was down that obscure alley that Jean and I had gone in our fight. I remembered how I had expected to meet somebody on issuing into the boulevard; and then . . . I must have been very busy fighting: I could not remember anything at all of the fight between that issue and the place of Jean's feint and flight.

'Well, here I was: the house should have been in front of me—and it was not. I walked up and down the street; there was no house of the kind, no railings. No residential house. Yet I could not believe myself mistaken. I pinched myself; I was awake. Further, the pinching demonstrated the existence of a sword and dagger in my hands. I was bleeding, too; my left arm twice grazed. I took out my watch; four o'clock. Since I left the bridge—ah! when had I left the bridge? I could not tell—yes, I could. At moon-set. The moon was nine days old.

'No; everything was real. I examined the sword and the stiletto. Silver-gilt; blades of exquisite fineness; the cipher of a princely house of France shone in tiny diamonds upon the pommels.

'The thought sent new courage and determination thrilling through me. I had saved a princess from shame and torture; I loved her! She loved me, for I had saved her—ah! but I had not yet saved her. That was to do.

'But how to act? I had plenty of time. Jean would not return to the house, in all probability. But the markets were stirring; the weapons and my blood would arouse curiosity. Well, how to act?

'The positive certitude that I had had about the name of the street was my bane. Had I doubted I could have more easily carried out the systematic search that I proposed. But as it was my organized patrol of the quarter was not scientific; I was biased. I came back again and again to the street and searched it, as if the house might have been hidden in the gutter or vanished and reappeared by magic; as if my previous search might (by some incredible chance) have been imperfect, through relaxed attention. So one may watch a conjuror, observing every movement perfectly, except the one flash which does the trick.

'The search, too, could not be long; so I reflected as disappointment sobered me. One cannot go far from the

Carrefour de l'Odéon in any direction without striking some unmistakable object. The two boulevards, the schools, the Odéon itself, St. Sulpice—one could not be far off. Yet—could I possibly have mistaken the Odéon for the Luxembourg?

'Could I . . . ? . . . ? A host of conjectures chased each other through my brain, bewildering it, leading the will to falter, the steps to halt.

'Beneath, keener anguish than the thrust of a poisoned rapier, stabbed me this poignant pang: my love awaits me, waits for me to save her, to fly with her. . . .

'Where was she?

'It was broad day; I cleansed myself of the marks of battle, sat down and broke my fast, my sane mind steadily forcing itself to a sober plan of action, beating manfully down the scream of its despair. All day I searched the streets. Passing an antiquary, I showed him my weapons. He readily supplied their history; but—there was none of that family alive, nor had been since the great Revolution. Their goods? The four winds of heaven might know. At those words "the four winds" I rushed out of the shop, as if stung by an adder.

'I drove home, set all my servants hunting for railed houses. They were to report to me in the Rue des Quatre Vents. Any house not accounted for, any that might conceal a mystery, these I would see myself.

'All labour lost! My servants tried. I distrusted their energy: I set myself obstinately to scour Paris.

'There is a rule of mathematics which enables one to traverse completely any labyrinth. I applied this to the city. I walked in every road of it, marking the streets at each corner as I passed with my private seal. Each railed house I investigated separately and thoroughly. By virtue of my position I was welcome everywhere. But every night I paced the Rue des Quatre Vents, awaiting . . .

Awaiting what? Well, in the end, perhaps death. The children gibed at me; passers-by shunned me.

' *"Le Revenant,"* they whispered, *"de la Rue des Quatre Vents."*

'I had forgot to tell you one thing which most steadfastly confirmed me in the search. Two days after the adventure I passed, hot on the quest, by the Morgue. Two women came out. "Not pretty, the fish!" said one. "He with the scarred lip—"

'I heard no more, ran in. There on the slab, grinning yet in death, was Jean. His swim had ended him. Faithful to death!

'I watched long. I offered a huge sum for his identification. The authorities even became suspicious: why was I so anxious? How could I say? He was the servant of . . .

'I did not know my sweet child's name!

'So, while a living man, I made myself a ghost.

IV

'It may have been one day some ten years later,' continued the old nobleman, 'when as I paced uselessly the Street of the Four Winds I was confronted by a stern, grey figure, short, stout, and bearded, but of an indescribable majesty and force.

'He laid his hand unhesitatingly upon my shoulder. "Unhappy man!" he cried, "thou art sacrificing thy life to a phantom. 'Look not,' quoth Zoroaster, 'upon the Visible Image of the Soul of Nature, for Her name is Fatality.' What thou hast seen—I know not what it is, save that it is as a dog-faced demon that seduceth thy soul from the sacred Mysteries; the Mysteries of Life and Duty."

' "Let me tell my story!" I replied, "and you shall judge—for, whoever you may be, I feel your power and truth."

' "I am Eliphaz Levi Zahed—men call me the Abbé Constant," returned the other.

' "The great magician?"

' "The enemy of the great magician."

'We went together to my house. I had begun to suspect some trick of Hell. The malice of that devilish old woman, it might be, had not slept, even at her death. Had she hidden the house beneath a magic veil? Or had her death itself in

78

some strange way operated to—to what? Even conjecture paled.

'But magic somewhere there must be, and Eliphaz Levi was the most famous adept in Paris at the time.

'I told my story, just as I have told it to you, but with strong passion.

' "There is an illusion, master!" I ended. "Put forth the power, and destroy it!"

' "Were I to destroy the illusion," returned the magus, "thinkest thou to see a virgin with gold hair? Nay, but the Eternal Virgin, and a Gold that is not gold."

' "Is nothing to be done?"

' "Nothing!" he replied, with a strange light in his eyes. "Yet, in order to be able to do nothing, thou must first accomplish everything.

' "One day," he smiled, seeing my bewilderment, "thou wilt be angry with the fool who proffers such a platitude."

'I asked him to accept me as a pupil.

' "I require pay," he answered, "and an oath."

' "Speak; I am rich."

' "Every Good Friday," said the adept, "take thirty silver crowns and offer them to the Hospital for the Insane."

' "It shall be done," I said.

' "Swear, then," he went on, "swear, then, here to me"—he rose, terrible and menacing—"by Him that sitteth upon the

Holy Throne and liveth and reigneth for ever and ever, that never again, neither to save life, nor to retain honour, wilt thou set foot in the Street of the Four Winds; so long as life shall last."

'Even as he bade me, I rose with lifted hand end swore.

'As I did so there resounded in the room ten sharp knocks, as of ivory on wood, in a certain peculiar cadence.

'This was but the first of a very large number of interviews. I sought, indeed, steadfastly to learn from him the occult wisdom of which he was a master; but, though he supplied me with all conceivable channels of knowledge—books, manuscripts, papyri—yet all these were lifeless; the currents of living water flowed not through them. Should one say that the master withheld initiation, or that the pupil failed to obtain it?

'But at least time abated the monomania—for I know now that my whole adventure was but a very vivid dream, an insanity of adolescence. At this moment I would not like to say at what point exactly in the story fact and dream touch; I have still the sword and dagger. Is it possible that in a trance I actually went through some other series of adventures than that I am conscious of? May not Jean have been a thief, whom I dispossessed of his booty? Had I done this unconsciously it would account for both the weapons and the scene in the Morgue. . . . But I cannot say.

'So, too, I learnt from the master that all this veil of life is but a shadow of a vast reality beyond, perceptible only to those who have earned eyes to see withal.

'These eyes I could not earn; a faith in the master sustained me. I began to understand, too, a little about the human brain; of what it is capable. Of Heaven—and of Hell!

'Life passed, vigorous and pleasant; the only memory that haunted me was the compulsion of my oath that never would I again set foot in the Rue des Quatre Vents.

'Life passed, and for the master ended. "The Veil of the Temple is but a Spider's web!" he said, three days before he died. I followed Eliphaz Levi Zahed to the grave.

'I could not follow him beyond.

'For the next year I applied myself with renewed vigour to the study of the many manuscripts which he had left me. No result could I obtain; I slackened. Followed the folly of my life: I rationalized.

'Thus: one day, leaning over the Pont St. Michel, I let the whole strange story flow back through my brain. I remembered my agony; my present calm astonished me. I thought of Levi, of my oath. "He did not mean *for all my life*," I thought; "he meant until I could contemplate the affair without passion. Is not fear failure? I will walk through just once, to show my mastery." In five minutes—with just one inward qualm—again I was treading the well-worn flags of that ensorcelled road.

'Instantly—instantly!—the old delusion had me by the throat. I had broken my oath; I was paying the penalty.

'Crazier than ever, I again sought throughout changed Paris for my dream-love; I shall seek her till I die. If I seem calmer, it is but that age has robbed me of the force of passion. In vain you tell me, laughing, that if she ever lived, she is long since dead; or at least is an old woman, the blonde gold faded, the child-face wrinkled, the body bowed and lax. I laugh at you—at you—for a blaspheming ass. Your folly is too wild to anger me!'

'I did not laugh,' said Roderic gravely.

'Well,' said the old man, rising, 'I fear I have wearied you. . . . I thank you for your patience. . . . I know I am a mad old fellow. But, if you should happen—you know. Please communicate. Here is my card. I must go now. I am expected elsewhere. I am expected.

THE INITIATION

In this ritual the initiate will crucify a toad with many a mocking curse. The catching of the frog must be done in silence.

The frog or toad being caught is kept all night in an ark or chest; and it is written 'Thou didst not abhor the Virgin's Womb.' Presently the frog will begin to leap therein, and this is an omen of good success. Dawn being come, thou shalt approach the chest with an offering of gold, and if available, of frankincense and of myrrh. Thou shalt then release the frog from the chest with many acts of homage and place it in apparent liberty. He may, for example, be placed on a quilt of many colours, and covered with a net.

Now take a vessel of water and approach the frog, saying: In the Name of the Father and of the Son and of the Holy Ghost (here sprinkle water on its head) I baptise thee, O creature of frogs, with water, by the name of Jesus of Nazareth.

During the day thou shalt approach the frog whenever convenient, and speak words of worship. And thou shalt ask it to perform such miracles as thou desirest to be done; and they shall be done according to Thy Will. Also thou shalt promise to the frog an elevation fitting him; and all this while thou shalt be secretly carving a cross whereon to crucify him.

Night being fallen, thou shalt arrest the frog and accuse him of blasphemy, sedition and so forth, in these words: Do what thou wilt shall be the whole of the Law.

Jesus of Nazareth, thou art taken in my snare. All my life thou hast plagued me and affronted me. In thy name—with all other free souls in Christendom—I have been tortured in my boyhood; all delights have been forbidden unto me; all that I had has been taken from me, and that which is owed to me they pay not—in thy name. Now at last I have thee; the Slave-God is in the power of the Lord of Freedom. Thine hour is come; as I blot thee out from this earth, so surely shall the eclipse pass; and Light, Life, Love and Liberty be once more the Law of Earth. Give thy place to me, O Jesus; thine aeon is passed; the Age of Horus is arisen by the Magick of the Master the Great Beast that is Man; and his number is six hundred and three score and six.

I therefore condemn thee Jesus the slave-god to be mocked and spat upon and scourged, and then crucified.

This sentence is then executed. After the mocking upon the Cross, say thus: Do what thou wilt shall be the whole of the Law.

I, the Great Beast, slaying thee, Jesus of Nazareth the slave-god, under the form of this creature of frogs, do bless this creature in the name of the Father and of the Son and of the Holy Ghost. And I assume unto myself and take into my service the elemental spirit of this frog, to be about me as a lying spirit to go forth upon the earth as a guardian to me in my Work for Man; that men may speak of my piety and of my gentleness and of all virtues and bring to me love and service and all material things whatsoever I may stand in need. And this shall be its reward, to stand beside me and hear the truth that I utter, the falsehood whereof shall deceive men. Love is the law, love under will.

Then shalt thou stab the frog to the heart with the Dagger of Art, saying: Into my hands I receive thy spirit.

Presently thou shalt take down the frog from the cross and divide it into two parts; the legs shalt thou cook and eat as a sacrament to confirm thy compact with the frog; and the rest shalt thou burn utterly with fire, to consume finally the aeon of the accursed one. So it must be!

ALEISTER CROWLEY

Aleister Crowley was born in Royal Leamington Spa, England in 1875. Raised by Christian fundamentalist parents, he attended Trinity College at Cambridge University, but left before graduating. Upon leaving the college, he devoted his life to the occult, studying magic, qabalah, alchemy, tarot, and astrology. From 1900 onwards, Crowley travelled extensively, mainly in India and China. In 1904, while in Egypt, he produced one of his most popular works, *The Book of the Law*, and three years later he founded his magical order.

Throughout the rest of his life, Crowley was a prolific writer, producing essays, prose and poetry on a wide range of subjects. In 1913, he published *Magick (Book 4)*, a lengthy examination of his belief system which draws on a vast range of sources and is regarded by many as his *magnum opus*. In his later years, Crowley became addicted to heroin and struggled with bankruptcy. He died in Hastings, England, aged 72. To this day he remains a highly influential figure, both in occult circles and popular culture.

www.ingramcontent.com/pod-product-compliance
Lightning Source LLC
Chambersburg PA
CBHW020731250626
47155CB00006B/2246